Welcome to The GROW & READ Early Reader Program!

The GROW & READ book program was developed under the supervision of reading specialists to develop kids' reading skills while emphasizing the delight of storytelling. The series was created to help children enjoy learning to read and is perfect for shared reading and reading aloud.

These GROW & READ levels will help you choose the best book for every reader.

GROW & READ
Developing Confidence for Success in Reading

1 GROW & READ
Level 1: Starting to Read (Preschool-Grade 1)
Simple sentences and easy sight words for growing confidence

2 GROW & READ
Level 2: Reading with Help (Grades 1-2)
Longer text, problem solving and growing vocabulary

3 GROW & READ
Level 3: Reading Independently (Grades 2-3)
More complex plots, feeding imagination and growing information skills

For more information visit growandread.com.

Published by Fabled Films LLC, New York

ISBN: 978-1-944020-30-9

Library of Congress Control Number: 2019939138

First Edition: October 2019

1 3 5 7 9 10 8 6 4 2

Cover Designed by Jaime Mendola-Hobbie
Jacket & Interior Art by Josie Yee
Interior Book Design by Aleks Gulan
Typeset in Stemple Garamond, Mrs. Ant and Pacific Northwest
Printed by Everbest in China

FABLED FILMS PRESS
NEW YORK CITY
fabledfilms.com

For information on bulk purchases for promotional use, please contact Consortium Book Sales & Distribution Sales department at ingrampublishersvcs@ingramcontent.com or 1-866-400-5351.

The
Tasty Treat

by

Tracey Hecht

Illustrations by
Josie Yee

Fabled Films Press
New York

Chapter 1

The moon was up.

The stars were twinkling.

It was nighttime.

But some animals were awake....

One of them was a fox.
The fox's name was Dawn.

Dawn was nocturnal,
awake at night,
and asleep in the day.

Dawn looked left.

Dawn looked right.

Where were her friends?
They were nocturnal, too.

"To-bin! Bis-mark!"

Dawn called out.

"Where are you?"

Dawn saw a tail.

The tail was long.

The tail was covered in scales.

The tail belonged to a pangolin!

Chapter 2

"There you are!" Dawn said.

The pangolin came out of the shrubs.

The pangolin's name was Tobin.

Tobin yawned.

Tobin stretched
his arms.

Tobin felt his tummy rumble!

"Oh goodness," Tobin said.

"I think I am hungry!"

"Why don't we look for a snack?"
Dawn said.

"And we can look for Bismark, too!"
Tobin added.

Suddenly, a greenish, round fruit dropped from the tree.

The fruit was a pomelo.

Then, a sugar glider dropped from the tree!

The sugar glider was Bismark.

Chapter 3

"Amigos!"

Bismark said to his friends.

"Look no further!

A snack and a sugar glider are here!"

Bismark had fancy flaps.

Bismark had
shiny silver fur.

Bismark had big black eyes,

and also a bit of a bald spot!

Tobin giggled.

Dawn's mouth turned up in a smile.

Bismark was not big,
but he was **bold**.

Bismark picked up the greenish, round fruit.

"Care for a bite?" Bismark asked.

"Oh goodness. Yes!" Tobin said.

"We can have a pomelo picnic," Dawn said.

Dawn peeled open the pomelo.

Dawn gave a piece to Tobin.

Dawn gave a piece to Bismark.

And the three nocturnal friends
shared a tasty treat!

The NOCTURNALS

FUN FACTS!

What Is a Nocturnal Animal?

Nocturnal
(NOK-tur-nel) *adjective*
Nocturnal animals are awake at night
and sleep during the day.

The Nocturnal Animal Friends in the Story

Pangolin
(PANG-guh-lin) *noun*
Pangolins have small, hard plates on
their bodies. They have long tongues but
no teeth. They are shy, and they make a
stinky smell or curl into a ball when they
are scared. They live in Asia and Africa,
but there are not many of them left in the
world. Many people are trying to protect
pangolins and the places where they live.

Red Fox
(RED FAHKS) *noun*
Red Foxes have yellow, orange,
or red fur and black feet. Their
big, bushy tails help to keep them
warm. They have very strong ears.
They can hear things that people
cannot! They live in cozy dens
with their parents when they are
young. When they are grown-ups,
they like to be alone. Foxes are
very smart, and they like to play.

Sugar Glider
(SHOO-ger GLAHY-der) *noun*

Sugar Gliders have small bodies, big eyes, and gray fur. When they are babies, they ride around in a special pocket on their mothers' bellies. They like to eat fruit and other sweet plants. Sugar gliders like to live in groups in tree branches. They cannot fly, but they can stretch out their bodies and float like a leaf from tree to tree.

What Is Their Nighttime Snack?

Pomelo
(POM-uh-loh) *noun*

Pomelos are fruits, and they grow on trees. They are round, and they look like grapefruits. On the outside, they are yellow or light green, and on the inside, they are pink and juicy. Tobin, Dawn, and Bismark love to eat this fruit! It is their favorite snack.

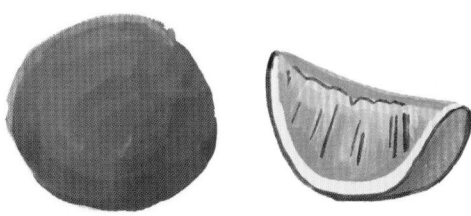

Grow & Read Storytime Activities
For The Nocturnals Early Reader Books!

Download Free Printables:

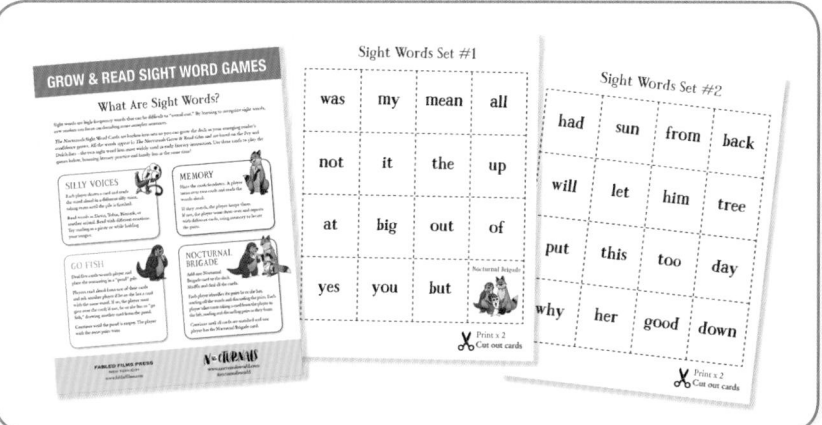

Sight Word Games

Brigade Mask Craft and Coloring Pages!

About the Author

Tracey Hecht is a writer and entrepreneur who has written, directed and produced for film. She created a Nocturnals Read Aloud Writing Program in partnership with the New York Public Library that has expanded nationwide. Tracey splits her time between Oquossoc, Maine and New York City.

About the Illustrator

Josie Yee is an award-winning illustrator and graphic artist specializing in children's publishing. She received her BFA from Arizona State University and studied Illustration at the Academy of Art University in San Francisco. She lives in New York City with her daughter, Ana, and their cat, Dude.

About Fabled Films

Fabled Films is a publishing and entertainment company creating original content for young readers and middle grade audiences. Fabled Films Press combines strong literary properties with high quality production values to connect books with generations of parents and their children. Each property is supported with additional content in the form of animated web series and social media as well as websites featuring activities for children, parents, bookstores, educators and librarians.

fabledfilms.com

FABLED FILMS PRESS
NEW YORK CITY

Read All of The Grow & Read Nocturnal Brigade Adventures!

This series can help children enjoy learning to read and is perfect for shared reading and reading aloud.

Great For Kids Ages 5-7

Level 1

Level 2

Level 3

Visit nocturnalsworld.com to download fun nighttime activities
#NocturnalsWorld